Scaredy

BOO!

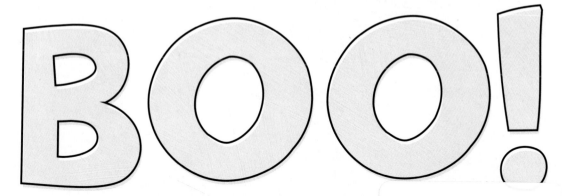

This edition published by Parragon Books Ltd in 2017

Parragon Books Ltd
Chartist House
15–17 Trim Street
Bath BA1 1HA, UK
www.parragon.com

Written by Claire Freedman   Illustrated by Russell Julian
Edited by Laura Baker   Designed by Kaye Hunter
Production by Richard Wheeler

ISBN 978-1-4748-6684-2

Printed in China

Scaredy
BOO!

Bath • New York • Cologne • Melbourne • Delhi
Hong Kong • Shenzhen • Singapore

Under the bed lived a monster,
A monster named **Scaredy Boo**.
Boo was afraid of everything.
He would have been scared of you!

Each night, the other small monsters
Raced round the house having fun.
Though all the children were sleeping,
Boo feared they'd **WAKE UP** someone!

Boo sighed, "I'm frightened of **Big** Things.

Small Things and Wiggly Things too!

I'm little Scaredy Boo monster.

Wouldn't these things scare YOU?"

Scaredy Boo didn't like noises,
Things that went crackle or *squeak*.
Hearing strange whispers and rustles
Made poor Boo's legs go all weak!

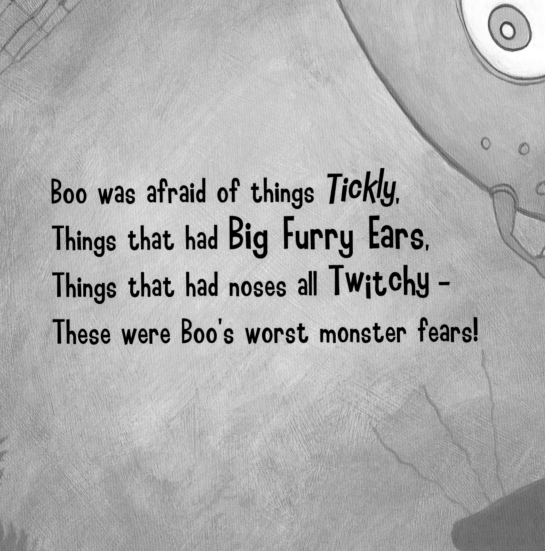

Boo was afraid of things *Tickly*,
Things that had Big Furry Ears,
Things that had noses all Twitchy –
These were Boo's worst monster fears!

Late one night, Boo heard **loud** footsteps.
"**Help!** Something's out there!" he said.
"Hello," the Thing called. "You hiding?"
It peeked at Boo under the bed.

Scaredy Boo trembled, "Who are you?
I jump when someone shouts BOO!
I'm little Scaredy Boo monster.
Wouldn't YOU be scared too?"

"Why are you scared?" smiled the stranger.
"I'm Spike – a monster like you!
Come out, and let's **play** together.
Playing's what monsters do!"

Poor Boo felt ever so worried.
He'd never been out before.
Night-time was all **dark** and **scary!**
Creakity-creak, creaked the floor.

"Come on!" Spike called to Boo kindly.
"Let's play with all of these toys!"
"Shh!" Scaredy whispered. "THE CHILDREN!
You'll wake them with all of the noise!"

Boo saw a huge **BLACK SHAPE** looming!
Oh, what a horrible sight!
"**Help!**" he cried, diving for cover.
There he sat, shaking with fright.

Scaredy Boo stuttered, "Wh-hat is that?
I jump when someone shouts BOO!
I'm little Scaredy Boo monster.
Wouldn't YOU be scared too?"

"That's just your shadow!" Spike told Boo.
"Everything has one – look, see?"
Scaredy Boo felt a little bit silly:
"All I was scared of was **ME!**"

Just then Boo stopped with a quiver.
"Wh-what's that?" he pointed with fear.
"Big-eared and floppy and furry!
It's much too scary around here!"

"That's just a teddy bear!" Spike said.
Boo asked him, "Do teddies bite?"
"No!" Spike laughed. "Teddies are **friendly!**
They love to cuddle at night!"

"**Help!** There's a Twitchy Thing!" Boo gasped.
Spike grinned, "It's only a **MOUSE!**"
"Oooh! It's quite friendly!" Boo giggled.
"I like exploring this house!"

Scaredy Boo met **ALL** of the monsters.
"It's so much fun playing," he said.
"Thank you, Spike – I'm glad you found me.
It's lonely under the bed!"

WHEEE! From a shelf dropped a spider.
Scaredy Boo's fur stood on end!
"I still don't like spiders!" Boo giggled.
"They scare me too!" laughed his friend.

Boo shouted, "Let's play tomorrow!
It's so *exciting* and *new*!"
"Shh!" all his monster friends whispered.
"YOU'RE NOISY NOW, LITTLE BOO!"